Nobody outfoxes Fantastic Mr. Fox!

Someone's been stealing from the three meanest farmers around, and they know the identity of the thief—it's Fantastic Mr. Fox! Working alone they could never catch him; but now fat Boggis, squat Bunce, and skinny Bean have joined forces, and they have Mr. Fox and his family surrounded. What they don't know is that they're not dealing with just any fox—Mr. Fox would rather die than surrender. Only the most fantastic plan can save him now.

Puffin Books by Roald Dahl

FANTASTIC
MR. FOX

ROALD DAHL

FANTASTIC MR. FOX

Illustrated by Quentin Blake

PUFFIN BOOKS

PUFFIN BOOKS
An imprint of Penguin Random House LLC
375 Hudson Street
New York, New York 10014

First published in the United States of America by Alfred A. Knopf, Inc., 1970
Published by Puffin Books by arrangement with Alfred A. Knopf, Inc., 1988
Reissued in this edition by Puffin Books, an imprint of
Penguin Young Readers Group, 2007, 2013

CIP DATA IS AVAILABLE

Puffin Books ISBN 978-0-14-241034-9

Printed in the United States of America

35 37 39 40 38 36 34

To Olivia

CONTENTS

FANTASTIC MR. FOX

1
The Three Farmers

DOWN IN THE VALLEY there were three farms. The owners of these farms had done well. They were rich men. They were also nasty men. All three of them were about as nasty and mean as any men you could meet. Their names were Farmer Boggis, Farmer Bunce and Farmer Bean.

Boggis was a chicken farmer. He kept thousands of chickens. He was enormously fat. This was because he ate three boiled chickens smothered with dumplings every day for breakfast, lunch and supper.

Bunce was a duck-and-goose farmer. He kept thousands of ducks and geese. He was a kind of pot-bellied dwarf. He was so short his chin would have been under water in the shallow end of any swimming-pool in the world. His food was dough-nuts and goose livers. He mashed the livers into a disgusting paste and then stuffed the paste into the doughnuts. This diet gave him a tummy-ache and a beastly temper.

Bean was a turkey-and-apple farmer. He kept thousands of turkeys in an orchard full of apple trees. He never ate any food at all. Instead, he drank gallons of strong cider which he made from the apples in his orchard. He was as thin as a pencil and the cleverest of them all.

Boggis and Bunce and Bean
One fat, one short, one lean.
These horrible crooks
So different in looks
Were nonetheless equally mean.

That is what the children round about used to sing when they saw them.

2
Mr. Fox

ON A HILL above the valley there was a wood.

In the wood there was a huge tree.

Under the tree there was a hole.

In the hole lived Mr. Fox and Mrs. Fox and their four Small Foxes.

Every evening as soon as it got dark, Mr. Fox would say to Mrs. Fox, "Well, my darling, what shall it be this time? A plump chicken from Boggis? A duck or a goose from Bunce? Or a nice turkey from Bean?" And when Mrs. Fox had told him what she wanted, Mr. Fox would creep down into the valley in the darkness of the night and help himself.

Boggis and Bunce and Bean knew very well what was going on, and it made them wild with rage. They were not men who liked to give anything away. Less still did they like anything to be stolen from them. So every night each of them would take his shotgun and hide in a dark place somewhere on his own farm, hoping to catch the robber.

But Mr. Fox was too clever for them. He always approached a farm with the wind blowing in his face, and this meant that if any man were lurking in the shadows ahead, the wind would carry the smell of that man to Mr. Fox's nose from far away. Thus, if Mr. Boggis was hiding behind his Chicken House Number One, Mr. Fox would smell him out from fifty yards off and quickly change direction, heading for Chicken House Number Four at the other end of the farm.

"Dang and blast that lousy beast!" cried Boggis.

"I'd like to rip his guts out!" said Bunce.

"He must be killed!" cried Bean.

"But how?" said Boggis. "How on earth can we catch the blighter?"

Bean picked his nose delicately with a long finger. "I have a plan," he said.

"You've never had a decent plan yet," said Bunce.

"Shut up and listen," said Bean. "Tomorrow night we will all hide just outside the hole where the fox lives. We will wait there until he comes out. Then . . . *Bang! Bang-bang-bang*."

"Very clever," said Bunce. "But first we shall have to find the hole."

"My dear Bunce, I've already found it," said the crafty Bean. "It's up in the wood on the hill. It's under a huge tree . . ."

3

The Shooting

"WELL, MY DARLING," said Mr. Fox. "What shall it be tonight?"

"I think we'll have duck tonight," said Mrs. Fox.

"Bring us two fat ducks, if you please. One for you and me, and one for the children."

"Ducks it shall be!" said Mr. Fox. "Bunce's best!"

"Now do be careful," said Mrs. Fox.

"My darling," said Mr. Fox, "I can smell those goons a mile away. I can even smell one from the other. Boggis gives off a filthy stink of rotten chicken-skins. Bunce reeks of goose-livers, and as for Bean, the fumes of apple cider hang around him like poisonous gases."

"Yes, but just don't get careless," said Mrs. Fox. "You know they'll be waiting for you, all three of them."

"Don't you worry about me," said Mr. Fox. "I'll see you later."

But Mr. Fox would not have been quite so cocky had he known exactly *where* the three farmers were waiting at that moment. They were just outside the entrance to the hole, each one crouching behind a tree with his gun loaded. And what is more, they had chosen their positions very carefully, making sure that the wind was not blowing from them towards the fox's hole. In fact, it was blowing in the opposite direction. There was no chance of them being "smelled out."

Mr. Fox crept up the dark tunnel to the mouth of his hole. He poked his long handsome face out into the night air and sniffed once.

He moved an inch or two forward and stopped.

He sniffed again. He was always especially careful when coming out from his hole.

He inched forward a little more. The front half of his body was now in the open.

His black nose twitched from side to side, sniffing and sniffing for the scent of danger. He found none, and he was just about to go trotting forward into the wood when he heard or thought he heard a tiny noise, a soft rustling sound, as though someone had moved a foot ever so gently through a patch of dry leaves.

Mr. Fox flattened his body against the ground and lay very still, his ears pricked. He waited a long time, but he heard nothing more.

"It must have been a field-mouse," he told himself, "or some other small animal."

He crept a little further out of the hole . . . then further still. He was almost right out in the open now. He took a last careful look around. The wood was murky and very still. Somewhere in the sky the moon was shining.

Just then, his sharp night-eyes caught a glint of something bright behind a tree not far away. It was a small silver speck of moonlight shining on a polished surface. Mr. Fox lay still, watching it. What on earth was it? Now it was moving. It was coming up and up . . . *Great heavens! It was the barrel of a gun!* Quick as a whip, Mr. Fox jumped back into his hole and at that same instant the entire wood seemed to explode around him. *Bang-bang! Bang-bang! Bang-bang!*

The smoke from the three guns floated upward in the night air. Boggis and Bunce and Bean came out from behind their trees and walked towards the hole.

"Did we get him?" said Bean.

One of them shone a flashlight on the hole, and there on the ground, in the circle of light, half in and half out of the hole, lay the poor tattered blood-stained remains of . . . a fox's tail. Bean picked it up. "We got the tail but we missed the fox," he said, toss-ing the thing away.

"Dang and blast!" said Boggis. "We shot too late. We should have let fly the moment he poked his head out."

"He won't be poking it out again in a hurry," Bunce said.

Bean pulled a flask from his pocket and took a swig of cider. Then he said, "It'll take three days at least before he gets hungry enough to come out again. I'm not sitting around here waiting for that. Let's dig him out."

"Ah," said Boggis. "Now you're talking sense. We can dig him out in a couple of hours. We know he's there."

"I reckon there's a whole family of them down that hole," Bunce said.

"Then we'll have the lot," said Bean. "Get the shovels!"

4
The Terrible Shovels

DOWN THE HOLE, Mrs. Fox was tenderly licking the stump of Mr. Fox's tail to stop the bleeding. "It was the finest tail for miles around," she said between licks.

"It hurts," said Mr. Fox.

"I know it does, sweetheart. But it'll soon get better."

"And it will soon grow again, Dad," said one of the Small Foxes.

"It will never grow again," said Mr. Fox. "I shall be tail-less for the rest of my life." He looked very glum.

There was no food for the foxes that night, and soon the children dozed off. Then Mrs. Fox dozed off. But Mr. Fox couldn't sleep because of the pain in the stump of his tail. "Well," he thought, "I suppose I'm lucky to be alive at all. And now they've found our hole, we're going to have to move out as soon as possible. We'll never get any peace if we . . . What was *that*?" He turned his head sharply and listened. The noise he heard now was the most frightening noise a fox can ever hear—the scrape-scrape-scraping of shovels digging into the soil.

"Wake up!" he shouted. "They're digging us out!"

Mrs. Fox was wide awake in one second. She sat up, quivering all over. "Are you sure that's it?" she whispered.

"I'm positive! Listen!"

"They'll kill my children!" cried Mrs. Fox.

"Never!" said Mr. Fox.

"But darling, they will!" sobbed Mrs. Fox. "You know they will!"

Scrunch, scrunch, scrunch went the shovels above their heads. Small stones and bits of earth began falling from the roof of the tunnel.

"How will they kill us, Mummy?" asked one of the Small Foxes. His round black eyes were huge with fright. "Will there be dogs?" he said.

Mrs. Fox began to cry. She gathered her four children close to her and held them tight.

Suddenly there was an especially loud crunch above their heads and the sharp end of a shovel came right through the ceiling. The sight of this awful thing seemed to have an electric effect upon Mr. Fox. He jumped up and shouted, "I've got it! Come on! There's not a moment to lose! Why didn't I think of it before!"

"Think of what, Dad?"

"A fox can dig quicker than a man!" shouted Mr. Fox, beginning to dig. "Nobody in the world can dig as quick as a fox!"

The soil began to fly out furiously behind Mr. Fox

as he started to dig for dear life with his front feet. Mrs. Fox ran forward to help him. So did the four children.

"Go downwards!" ordered Mr. Fox. "We've got to go deep! As deep as we possibly can!"

The tunnel began to grow longer and longer. It sloped steeply downward. Deeper and deeper below the surface of the ground it went. The mother and the father and all four of the children were digging together. Their front legs were moving so fast you couldn't see them. And gradually the scrunching and scraping of the shovels became fainter and fainter.

After about an hour, Mr. Fox stopped digging. "Hold it!" he said. They all stopped. They turned and looked back up the long tunnel they had just dug. All was quiet. "Phew!" said Mr. Fox. "I think we've done it! They'll never get as deep as this. Well done, everyone!"

They all sat down, panting for breath. And Mrs. Fox said to her children, "I should like you to know that if it wasn't for your father we should all be dead by now. Your father is a fantastic fox."

Mr. Fox looked at his wife and she smiled. He loved her more than ever when she said things like that.

5
The Terrible Tractors

As THE SUN ROSE the next morning, Boggis and Bunce and Bean were still digging. They had dug a hole so deep you could have put a house into it. But they had not yet come to the end of the fox's tunnel. They were all very tired and cross.

"Dang and blast!" said Boggis. "Whose rotten idea was this?"

"Bean's idea," said Bunce.

Boggis and Bunce both stared at Bean. Bean took another swig of cider, then put the flask back into his pocket without offering it to the others. "Listen," he said angrily, "I want that fox! I'm going to get that fox! I'm not giving in till I've strung him up over my front porch, dead as a dumpling!"

"We can't get him by digging, that's for sure," said the fat Boggis. "I've had enough of digging."

Bunce, the little pot-bellied dwarf, looked up at Bean and said, "Have you got any more stupid ideas, then?"

"What?" said Bean. "I can't hear you." Bean never took a bath. He never even washed. As a result, his earholes were clogged with all kinds of muck and wax and bits of chewing-gum and dead flies and stuff like that. This made him deaf. "Speak louder," he said to Bunce, and Bunce shouted back, "Got any more stupid ideas?"

Bean rubbed the back of his neck with a dirty finger. He had a boil coming there and it itched. "What we need on this job," he said, "is machines . . . *mechanical* shovels. We'll have him out in five minutes with *mechanical* shovels."

This was a pretty good idea and the other two had to admit it.

"All right then," Bean said, taking charge. "Boggis, you stay here and see the fox doesn't escape. Bunce and I will go and fetch our machinery. If he tries to get out, shoot him quick."

The long, thin Bean walked away. The tiny Bunce trotted after him. The fat Boggis stayed where he was with his gun pointing at the fox-hole.

Soon, two enormous caterpillar tractors with mechanical shovels on their front ends came clanking into the wood. Bean was driving one. Bunce the

other. The machines were
both black. They were murderous,
brutal-looking monsters.

"Here we go, then!" shouted Bean.

"Death to the fox!" shouted Bunce.

The machines went to work, biting huge mouth-
fuls of soil out of the hill. The big tree under which
Mr. Fox had dug his hole in the first place was toppled
like a matchstick. On all sides, rocks were sent flying
and trees were falling and the noise was deafening.

Down in the tunnel the foxes crouched, listening to the terrible clanging and banging overhead. "What's happening, Dad?" cried the Small Foxes. "What are they doing?"

Mr. Fox didn't know what was happening or what they were doing.

"It's an earthquake!" cried Mrs. Fox.

"Look!" said one of the Small Foxes. "Our tunnel's got shorter! I can see daylight!"

They all looked round, and yes, the mouth of the tunnel was only a few feet away from them now, and in the circle of daylight beyond they could see the two huge black tractors almost on top of them.

"Tractors!" shouted Mr. Fox. "And *mechanical* shovels! Dig for your lives! *Dig, dig, dig!*"

6
The Race

NOW THERE BEGAN a desperate race, the machines against the foxes. In the beginning, the hill looked like this:

After about an hour, as the machines bit away more and more soil from the hilltop, it looked like this:

Sometimes the foxes would gain a little ground and the clanking noises would grow fainter and Mr. Fox would say, "We're going to make it! I'm sure we are!" But then a few moments later, the machines would come back at them and the crunch of the mighty shovels would get louder and louder. Once the foxes actually saw the sharp metal edge of one of the shovels as it scraped up the earth just behind them.

"Keep going, my darlings!" panted Mr. Fox. "Don't give up!"

"Keep going!" the fat Boggis shouted to Bunce and Bean. "We'll get him any moment now!"

"Have you caught sight of him yet?" Bean called back.

"Not yet," shouted Boggis. "But I think you're close!"

"I'll pick him up with my bucket!" shouted Bunce. "I'll chop him to pieces!"

But by lunchtime the machines were still at it. And so were the poor foxes. The hill now looked like this:

The farmers didn't stop for lunch; they were too keen to finish the job.

"Hey there, Mr. Fox!" yelled Bunce, leaning out of his tractor. "We're coming to get you now!"

"You've had your last chicken!" yelled Boggis. "You'll never come prowling around *my* farm again!"

A sort of madness had taken hold of the three men. The tall skinny Bean and dwarfish pot-bellied Bunce were driving their machines like maniacs, racing the motors and making the shovels dig at a terrific speed. The fat Boggis was hopping about like a dervish and shouting, "Faster! Faster!"

By five o'clock in the afternoon this is what had happened to the hill:

The hole the machines had dug was like the crater of a volcano. It was such an extraordinary sight that crowds of people came rushing out from the surrounding villages to have a look. They stood on the edge of the crater and stared down at Boggis and Bunce and Bean.

"Hey there, Boggis! What's going on?"

"We're after a fox!"

"You must be mad!"

The people jeered and laughed. But this only made the three farmers more furious and more obstinate and more determined than ever not to give up until they had caught the fox.

7

"We'll Never Let Him Go"

AT SIX O'CLOCK in the evening, Bean switched off the motor of his tractor and climbed down from the driver's seat. Bunce did the same. Both men had had enough. They were tired and stiff from driving the tractors all day. They were also hungry. Slowly they walked over to the small fox's hole in the bottom of the huge crater. Bean's face was purple with rage. Bunce was cursing the fox with dirty words that cannot be printed. Boggis came waddling up. "Dang and blast that filthy stinking fox!" he said. "What the heck do we do now?"

"I'll tell you what we *don't* do," Bean said. "We don't let him go!"

"We'll never let him go!" Bunce declared.

"Never never never!" cried Boggis.

"Did you hear that, Mr. Fox!" yelled Bean, bending low and shouting down the hole. "It's not over yet, Mr. Fox! We're not going home till we've strung you up dead as a dingbat!" Whereupon the three men all shook hands with one another and swore a solemn oath that they would not go back to their farms until the fox was caught.

"What's the next move?" asked Bunce, the pot-bellied dwarf.

"We're sending you down the hole to fetch him up," said Bean. "Down you go, you miserable midget!"

"Not me!" screamed Bunce, running away.

Bean made a sickly smile. When he smiled you saw his scarlet gums. You saw more gums than teeth. "Then there's only one thing to do," he said. "We starve him out. We camp here day and night watching the hole. He'll come out in the end. He'll have to."

So Boggis and Bunce and Bean sent messages down to their farms asking for tents, sleeping-bags and supper.

8

The Foxes Begin to Starve

THAT EVENING three tents were put up in the crater on the hill—one for Boggis, one for Bunce and one for Bean. The tents surrounded Mr. Fox's hole. And the three farmers sat outside their tents eating their supper. Boggis had three boiled chickens smothered in dumplings, Bunce had six doughnuts filled with disgusting goose-liver paste, and Bean had two gallons of cider. All three of them kept their guns beside them.

Boggis picked up a steaming chicken and held it close to the fox's hole. "Can you smell this, Mr. Fox?" he shouted. "Lovely tender chicken! Why don't you come up and get it?"

The rich scent of chicken wafted down the tunnel to where the foxes were crouching.

"Oh, Dad," said one of the Small Foxes, "couldn't we just sneak up and snatch it out of his hand?"

"Don't you dare!" said Mrs. Fox. "That's just what they want you to do."

"But we're so *hungry!*" they cried. "How long will it be till we get something to eat?"

Their mother didn't answer them. Nor did their father. There was no answer to give.

As darkness fell, Bunce and Bean switched on the powerful headlamps of the two tractors and shone them on to the hole. "Now," said Bean, "we'll take it in turn to keep watch. One watches while two sleep, and so on all through the night."

Boggis said, "What if the fox digs a hole right through the hill and comes out on the other side? You didn't think of that one, did you?"

"Of course I did," said Bean, pretending he had.

"Go on, then, tell us the answer," said Boggis.

Bean picked something small and black out of his ear and flicked it away. "How many men have you got working on your farm?" he asked.

"Thirty-five," Boggis said.

"I've got thirty-six," Bunce said.

"And I've got thirty-seven," Bean said. "That makes one hundred and eight men altogether. We must order them to surround the hill. Each man will have a gun and a flashlight. There will be no escape then for Mr. Fox."

So the order went down to the farms, and that night one hundred and eight men formed a tight ring around the bottom of the hill. They were armed with sticks and guns and hatchets and pistols and all sorts of other horrible weapons. This made it quite impossible for a fox or indeed for any other animal to escape from the hill.

The next day, the watching and waiting went on. Boggis and Bunce and Bean sat upon small stools, staring at the fox's hole. They didn't talk much. They just sat there with their guns on their laps.

Every so often, Mr. Fox would creep a little closer towards the mouth of the tunnel and take a sniff. Then he would creep back again and say, "They're still there."

"Are you quite sure?" Mrs. Fox would ask.

"Positive," said Mr. Fox. "I can smell that man Bean a mile away. He stinks."

9
Mr. Fox Has a Plan

FOR THREE DAYS and three nights this waiting-game went on.

"How long can a fox go without food or water?" Boggis asked on the third day.

"Not much longer now," Bean told him. "He'll make a run for it soon. He'll have to."

Bean was right. Down in the tunnel the foxes were slowly but surely starving to death.

"If only we could have just a tiny sip of water," said one of the Small Foxes. "Oh, Dad, can't you do *something*?"

"Couldn't we make a dash for it, Dad? We'd have a little bit of a chance, wouldn't we?"

"No chance at all," snapped Mrs. Fox. "I refuse to

let you go up there and face those guns. I'd sooner
you stay down here and die in peace."

Mr. Fox had not spoken for a long time. He had
been sitting quite still, his eyes closed, not even hear-
ing what the others were saying. Mrs. Fox knew that
he was trying desperately to think of a way out.
And now, as she looked at him, she saw him stir himself and get slowly to his feet. He looked back at his
wife. There was a little spark of excitement dancing
in his eyes.

"What is it, darling?" said Mrs. Fox quickly.

"I've just had a bit of an idea," Mr. Fox said carefully.

"What?" they cried. "Oh, Dad, what is it?"

"Come *on!*" said Mrs. Fox. "Tell us quickly!"

"Well . . ." said Mr. Fox, then he stopped and
sighed and sadly shook his head. He sat down again.
"It's no good," he said. "It won't work after all."

"Why not, Dad?"

"Because it means more digging and we aren't any of us strong enough for that after three days and nights without food."

"Yes we are, Dad!" cried the Small Foxes, jumping up and running to their father. "We can do it! You see if we can't! So can you!"

Mr. Fox looked at the four Small Foxes and he smiled. What fine children I have, he thought. They are starving to death and they haven't had a drink for three days, but they are still undefeated. I must not let them down.

"I . . . I suppose we could give it a try," he said.

"Let's go, Dad! Tell us what you want us to do!"

Slowly, Mrs. Fox got to her feet. She was suffering more than any of them from the lack of food and water. She was very weak. "I am so sorry," she said, "but I don't think I am going to be much help."

"You stay right where you are, my darling," said Mr. Fox. "We can handle this by ourselves."

10
Boggis's Chicken House
Number One

"THIS TIME we must go in a very special direction," said Mr. Fox, pointing sideways and downward.

So he and his four children started to dig once again. The work went much more slowly now. Yet they kept at it with great courage, and little by little the tunnel began to grow.

"Dad, I wish you would tell us *where* we are going," said one of the children.

"I dare not do that," said Mr. Fox, "because this place I am *hoping* to get to is so *marvellous* that if I described it to you now you would go crazy with excitement. And then, if we failed to get there (which is very possible), you would die of disappointment. I don't want to raise your hopes too much, my darlings."

For a long long time they kept on digging. For how long they did not know, because there were no days and no nights down there in the murky tunnel. But at last Mr. Fox gave the order to stop. "I think," he said, "we had better take a peep upstairs now and see where we are. I know where I *want* to be, but I can't possibly be sure we're anywhere near it."

Slowly, wearily, the foxes began to slope the tunnel up towards the surface. Up and up it went . . . until suddenly they came to something hard above their heads and they couldn't go up any further. Mr. Fox reached up to examine this hard thing. "It's wood!" he whispered. "Wooden planks!"

"What does that mean, Dad?"

"It means, unless I am very much mistaken, that we are right underneath somebody's house," whispered Mr. Fox. "Be very quiet now while I take a peek."

Carefully, Mr. Fox began pushing up one of the floorboards. The board creaked most terribly and they all ducked down, waiting for something awful to happen. Nothing did. So Mr. Fox pushed up a second board. And then, very very cautiously, he poked his head up through the gap. He let out a shriek of excitement.

"I've done it!" he yelled. "I've done it *first time!* *I've done it! I've done it!*" He pulled himself up through the gap in the floor and started prancing and dancing with joy. "Come on up!" he sang out. "Come up and see where you are, my darlings! What a sight for a hungry fox! Hallelujah! Hooray! Hooray!"

The four Small Foxes scrambled up out of the tunnel and what a fantastic sight it was that now met their eyes! They were in a huge shed and the whole place was teeming with chickens. There were white chickens and brown chickens and black chickens by the thousand!

"Boggis's Chicken House Number One!" cried Mr. Fox. "It's exactly what I was aiming at! I hit it slap in the middle! First time! Isn't that fantastic! *And,* if I may say so, rather clever!"

The Small Foxes went wild with excitement. They started running around in all directions, chasing the stupid chickens.

"Wait!" ordered Mr. Fox. "Don't lose your heads! Stand back! Calm down! Let's do this properly! First of all, everyone have a drink of water!"

They all ran over to the chickens' drinking-trough and lapped up the lovely cool water. Then Mr. Fox chose three of the plumpest hens, and with a clever flick of his jaws he killed them instantly.

"Back to the tunnel!" he ordered. "Come on! No

fooling around! The quicker you move, the quicker you shall have something to eat!"

One after another, they climbed down through the hole in the floor and soon they were all standing once again in the dark tunnel. Mr. Fox reached up and pulled the floorboards back into place. He did this with great care. He did it so that no one could tell they had ever been moved.

"My son," he said, giving the three plump hens to the biggest of his four small children, "run back with these to your mother. Tell her to prepare a feast. Tell her the rest of us will be along in a jiffy, as soon as we have made a few other little arrangements."

11
A Surprise for Mrs. Fox

THE SMALL FOX ran back along the tunnel as fast as he could, carrying the three plump hens. He was exploding with joy. "Just wait!" he kept thinking, "just wait till Mummy sees these!" He had a long way to run but he never stopped once on the way and he came bursting in upon Mrs. Fox. "Mummy!" he cried, out of breath. "Look, Mummy, look! Wake up and see what I've brought you!"

Mrs. Fox, who was weaker than ever now from lack of food, opened one eye and looked at the hens. "I'm dreaming," she murmured and closed the eye again.

"You're not dreaming, Mummy! They're real chickens! We're saved! We're not going to starve!"

Mrs. Fox opened both eyes and sat up quickly. "But, my *dear* child!" she cried. "Where on earth . . . ?"

"Boggis's Chicken House Number One!" spluttered the Small Fox. "We tunnelled right up under the floor and you've never seen so many big fat hens in all your life! And Dad said to prepare a feast! They'll be back soon!"

The sight of food seemed to give new strength to Mrs. Fox. "A feast it shall be!" she said, standing up. "Oh, what a fantastic fox your father is! Hurry up, child, and start plucking those chickens!"

Far away down in the tunnel, the fantastic Mr. Fox was saying, "Now for the next bit, my darlings! This one'll be as easy as pie! All we have to do is dig another little tunnel from *here* to there!"

"To where, Dad?"

"Don't ask so many questions. Start digging!"

12
Badger

MR. FOX and the three remaining Small Foxes dug fast and straight. They were all too excited now to feel tired or hungry. They knew they were going to have a whacking great feast before long and the fact that it was none other than Boggis's chickens they were going to eat made them churgle with laughter every time they thought of it. It was lovely to realize that while the fat farmer was sitting up there on the hill waiting for them to starve, he was also giving them their dinner without knowing it. "Keep digging," said Mr. Fox. "It's not much further."

All of a sudden a deep voice above their heads said, *"Who goes there?"* The foxes jumped. They looked up quickly and they saw, peeking through a small hole in the roof of the tunnel, a long black pointed furry face.

"Badger!" cried Mr. Fox.

"Foxy!" cried Badger. "My goodness me, I'm glad I've found *someone* at last! I've been digging around in circles for three days and nights and I haven't the foggiest idea where I am!"

Badger made the hole in the ceiling bigger and dropped down beside the foxes. A Small Badger (his son) dropped down after him. "Haven't you *heard* what's happening up on the hill?" Badger said excitedly. "It's chaos! Half the wood has disappeared and there are men with guns all over the countryside! None of us can get out, even at night! We're all starving to death!"

"Who is *we*?" asked Mr. Fox.

"All us diggers. That's me and Mole and Rabbit and all our wives and children. Even Weasel, who can usually sneak out of the tightest spots, is right now hiding down my hole with Mrs. Weasel and six kids. What on earth are we going to do, Foxy? I think we're finished!"

Mr. Fox looked at his three children and he smiled. The children smiled back at him, sharing his secret. "My dear old Badger," he said, "this mess you're in is all my fault . . ."

"I *know* it's your fault!" said Badger furiously. "And the farmers are not going to give up till they've got you. Unfortunately, that means *us* as well. It means everyone on the hill." Badger sat down and put a paw around his small son. "We're done for," he said softly. "My poor wife up there is so weak she can't dig another yard."

"Nor can mine," said Mr. Fox. "And yet at this very minute she is preparing for me and my children the most delicious feast of plump juicy chickens . . ."

"Stop!" cried Badger. "Don't tease me! I can't stand it!"

"It's true!" cried the Small Foxes. "Dad's not teasing! We've got chickens galore!"

"And because everything is entirely my fault," said Mr. Fox, "I invite you to share the feast. I invite *everyone* to share it—you and Mole and Rabbit and Weasel and all your wives and children. There'll be plenty to go round, I can assure you."

"You mean it?" cried Badger. "You *really mean* it?"

Mr. Fox pushed his face close to Badger's and

whispered darkly, "*Do you know* where we've just been?"

"Where?"

"Right inside Boggis's Chicken House Number One!"

"No!"

"Yes! But that is nothing to where we are going now. You have come just at the right moment, my dear Badger. You can help us dig. And in the meanwhile, your small son can run back to Mrs. Badger and all the others and spread the good news." Mr. Fox turned to the Small Badger and said, "Tell them they are invited to a Fox's Feast. Then bring them all down here and follow this tunnel back until you find my home!"

"Yes, Mr. Fox!" said the Small Badger. "Yes, sir! Right away, sir! Oh, thank you, sir!" and he scrambled quickly back through the hole in the roof of the tunnel and disappeared.

13
Bunce's Giant Storehouse

"My DEAR FOXY!" cried Badger. "What in the world has happened to your tail?"

"Don't talk about it, *please*," said Mr. Fox. "It's a painful subject."

They were digging the new tunnel. They dug on in silence. Badger was a great digger and the tunnel went forward at a terrific pace now that he was lending a paw. Soon they were crouching underneath yet another wooden floor.

Mr. Fox grinned slyly, showing sharp white teeth. "If I am not mistaken, my dear Badger," he said, "we are now underneath the farm which belongs to that nasty little pot-bellied dwarf, Bunce. We are, in fact, directly underneath the most *interesting part* of that farm."

"Ducks and geese!" cried the Small Foxes, licking their lips. "Juicy tender ducks and big fat geese!"

"Ex-*actly!*" said Mr. Fox.

"But how in the world can you know where we are?" asked Badger.

Mr. Fox grinned again, showing even more white teeth. "Look," he said, "I know my way around these farms blindfold. For me it's just as easy below ground as it is above it." He reached high and pushed up one wooden floorboard, then another. He poked his head through the gap.

"Yes!" he shouted, jumping up into the room above. "I've done it again! I've hit it smack on the nose! Right in the bull's-eye! Come and look!"

Quickly Badger and the three Small Foxes scrambled up after him. They stopped and stared. They stood and gaped. They were so overwhelmed they couldn't speak; for what they now saw was a kind of fox's dream, a badger's dream, a paradise for hungry animals.

"This, my dear old Badger," proclaimed Mr. Fox, "is Bunce's Mighty Storehouse! All his finest stuff is stored in here before he sends it off to market."

Against all the four walls of the great room, stacked in cupboards and piled upon shelves reaching from floor to ceiling, were thousands and thousands of the finest and fattest ducks and geese, plucked and ready for roasting! And up above, dangling from the rafters, there must have been at least a hundred smoked hams and fifty sides of bacon!

"Just feast your eyes on *that!*" cried Mr. Fox, dancing up and down. "What d'you think of it, eh? Pretty good grub!"

Suddenly, as though springs had been released in their legs, the three hungry Small Foxes and the ravenously hungry Badger sprang forward to grab the luscious food.

"Stop!" ordered Mr. Fox. "This is *my* party, so *I* shall do the choosing." The others fell back, licking their chops. Mr. Fox began prowling around the storehouse examining the glorious display with an expert eye. A thread of saliva slid down one side of his jaw and hung suspended in mid-air, then snapped.

"We mustn't overdo it," he said. "Mustn't give the game away. Mustn't let them know what we've been up to. We must be neat and tidy and take just a few of the choicest morsels. So, to start with we shall have four plump young ducks." He took them from the shelf. "Oh, how lovely and fat they are! No wonder Bunce gets a special price for them in the market! . . . All right, Badger, lend me a hand to get them down . . . You children can help as well . . . There we go . . . Goodness me, look how your mouths are watering . . . And now . . . I think we had better have a few geese . . . Three will be quite enough . . . We'll take the biggest . . . Oh my, oh my, you'll never see finer geese than these in a king's kitchen . . . Gently does it . . . that's the way . . . And what about a couple of nice smoked hams . . . I adore smoked ham, don't you, Badger? . . . Fetch me that step-ladder, will you please . . ."

Mr. Fox climbed up the ladder and handed down

three magnificent hams. "And do you like bacon, Badger?"

"I'm mad about bacon!" cried Badger, dancing with excitement. "Let's have a side of bacon! That big one up there!"

"And carrots, Dad!" said the smallest of the three Small Foxes. "We must take some of those carrots."

"Don't be a twerp," said Mr. Fox. "You know we never eat things like that."

"It's not for us, Dad. It's for the Rabbits. They only eat vegetables."

"My goodness me, you're right!" cried Mr. Fox. "What a thoughtful little fellow you are! Take ten bunches of carrots!"

Soon, all this lovely loot was lying in a neat heap upon the floor. The Small Foxes crouched close, their noses twitching, their eyes shining like stars.

"And now," said Mr. Fox, "we shall have to borrow from our friend Bunce two of those useful push-carts over in the corner." He and Badger fetched the push-carts, and the ducks and geese and hams and bacon were loaded on to them. Quickly the push-carts were lowered through the hole in the floor. The animals slid down after them. Back in the tunnel, Mr. Fox again pulled the floorboards very carefully into place so that no one could see they had been moved.

"My darlings," he said, pointing to two of the three Small Foxes, "take a cart each and run back as fast as you can to your mother. Give her my love and tell her we are having guests for dinner—the Badgers, the Moles, the Rabbits and the Weasels. Tell her it must be a truly great feast. And tell her the rest of us will be home as soon as we've done one more little job."

"Yes, Dad! Right away, Dad!" they answered, and they grabbed a trolley each and went rushing off down the tunnel.

14
Badger Has Doubts

"JUST ONE MORE VISIT!" cried Mr. Fox.

"And I'll bet I know where that'll be," said the only Small Fox now left. He was the Smallest Fox of them all.

"Where?" said Badger.

"Well," said the Smallest Fox. "We've been to Boggis and we've been to Bunce but we haven't been to Bean. It must be Bean."

"You are right," said Mr. Fox. "But what you don't know is which *part* of Bean's place we are about to visit."

"Which?" they said both together.

"Ah-ha," said Mr. Fox. "Just you wait and see." They were digging as they talked. The tunnel was going forward fast.

Suddenly Badger said, "Doesn't this worry you just a tiny bit, Foxy?"

"Worry me?" said Mr. Fox. "What?"

"All this . . . this *stealing*."

Mr. Fox stopped digging and stared at Badger as though he had gone completely dotty. "My dear old furry frump," he said, "do you know anyone in the *whole world* who wouldn't swipe a few chickens if his children were starving to death?"

There was a short silence while Badger thought deeply about this.

"You are far too respectable," said Mr. Fox.

"There's nothing wrong with being respectable," Badger said.

"Look," said Mr. Fox, "Boggis and Bunce and Bean are out to *kill* us. You realize that, I hope?"

"I do, Foxy, I do indeed," said the gentle Badger.

"But *we're* not going to stoop to *their* level. We don't want to kill *them*."

"I should hope not, indeed," said Badger.

"We wouldn't dream of it," said Mr. Fox. "We shall simply take a little food here and there to keep us and our families alive. Right?"

"I suppose we'll have to," said Badger.

"If *they* want to be horrible, let them," said Mr. Fox. "We down here are decent peace-loving people."

Badger laid his head on one side and smiled at Mr. Fox. "Foxy," he said, "I love you."

"Thank you," said Mr. Fox. "And now let's get on with the digging."

Five minutes later, Badger's front paws hit against something flat and hard. "What on earth is this?" he said. "It looks like a solid stone wall." He and Mr. Fox scraped away the soil. It *was* a wall. But it was built of bricks, not stones. The wall was right in front of them, blocking their way.

"Now who in the world would build a wall under the ground?" asked Badger.

"Very simple," said Mr. Fox. "It's the wall of an underground room. And if I am not mistaken, it is exactly what I'm looking for."

15
Bean's Secret Cider Cellar

Mr. Fox examined the wall carefully. He saw that the cement between the bricks was old and crumbly, so he loosened a brick without much trouble and pulled it away. Suddenly, out from the hole where the brick had been, there popped a small sharp face with whiskers, "Go away!" it snapped. "You can't come in here! It's private!"

"Good Lord!" said Badger. "It's Rat!"

"You saucy beast!" said Mr. Fox. "I should have guessed we'd find you down here somewhere."

"Go away!" shrieked Rat. "Go on, beat it! This is my private pitch!"

"Shut up," said Mr. Fox.

"I will not shut up!" shrieked Rat. "This is *my* place! I got here first!"

Mr. Fox gave a brilliant smile, flashing his white teeth. "My dear Rat," he said softly, "I am a hungry fellow and if you don't hop it quickly I shall eat-you-up-in-one-gulp!"

That did it. Rat popped back fast out of sight. Mr. Fox laughed and began pulling more bricks out of the wall. When he had made a biggish hole, he crept through it. Badger and the Smallest Fox followed him in.

They found themselves in a vast, damp, gloomy cellar. "This is it!" cried Mr. Fox.

"This is *what*?" said Badger. "The place is empty."

"Where are the turkeys?" asked the Smallest Fox, staring into the gloom. "I thought Bean was a turkey man."

"He is a turkey man," said Mr. Fox. "But we're not after turkeys now. We've got plenty of food."

"Then what *do* we need, Dad?"

"Take a good look round," said Mr. Fox. "Don't you see *anything* that interests you?"

Badger and the Smallest Fox peered into the half-darkness. As their eyes became accustomed to the gloom, they began to see what looked like a whole lot of big glass jars standing upon shelves around the walls. They went closer. They *were* jars. There were hundreds of them, and upon each one was written the word CIDER.

The Smallest Fox leaped high in the air. "Oh, Dad!" he cried out. "Look what we've found! It's cider!"

"Ex-*actly*," said Mr. Fox.

"Tremendous!" shouted Badger.

"Bean's Secret Cider Cellar," said Mr. Fox. "But go carefully, my dears. Don't make a noise. This cellar is right underneath the farmhouse itself."

"Cider," said Badger, "is especially good for Badgers. We take it as medicine—one large glass three times a day with meals and another at bedtime."

"It will make the feast into a banquet," said Mr. Fox.

While they were talking, the Smallest Fox had sneaked a jar off the shelf and had taken a gulp. "Wow!" he gasped. "Wow-*ee!*"

You must understand this was not the ordinary weak fizzy cider one buys in a store. It was the real stuff, a home-brewed fiery liquor that burned in your throat and boiled in your stomach.

"Ah-h-h-h-h-h!" gasped the Smallest Fox. "This is *some cider!*"

"That's quite enough of that," said Mr. Fox, grabbing the jar and putting it to his own lips. He took a tremendous gulp. "It's miraculous!" he whispered, fighting for breath. "It's fabulous! It's beautiful!"

"It's my turn," said Badger, taking the jar and tilting his head well back. The cider gurgled and bubbled down his throat. "It's . . . it's like melted gold!" he gasped. "Oh, Foxy, it's . . . like drinking sunbeams and rainbows!"

"You're poaching!" shrieked Rat. "Put that down at once! There'll be none left for me!" Rat was perched upon the highest shelf in the cellar, peering out from behind a huge jar. There was a small rubber tube inserted in the neck of the jar, and Rat was using this tube to suck out the cider.

"You're drunk!" said Mr. Fox.

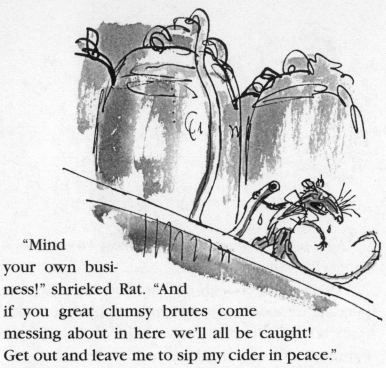

"Mind
your own busi-
ness!" shrieked Rat. "And
if you great clumsy brutes come
messing about in here we'll all be caught!
Get out and leave me to sip my cider in peace."

At that moment they heard a woman's voice calling out in the house above them. "Hurry up and get that cider, Mabel!" the voice called. "You know Mr. Bean doesn't like to be kept waiting! Especially when he's been out all night in a tent!"

The animals froze. They stayed absolutely still, their ears pricked, their bodies tense. Then they heard the sound of a door being opened. The door was at the top of a flight of stone steps leading down from the house to the cellar.

And now someone was starting to come down those steps.

16
The Woman

"QUICK!" SAID MR. FOX. "Hide!" He and Badger and the Smallest Fox jumped up on to a shelf and crouched behind a row of big cider jars. Peering around the jars, they saw a huge woman coming down into the cellar. At the foot of the steps, the woman paused, looking to right and left. Then she turned and headed straight for the place where Mr. Fox and Badger and the Smallest Fox were hiding. She stopped right in front of them. The only thing between her and them was a row of cider jars. She was so close, Mr. Fox could hear the sound of her breathing. Peeping through the crack between two bottles, he noticed that she carried a big rolling-pin in one hand.

"How many will he want this time, Mrs. Bean?" the woman shouted. And from the top of the steps the other voice called back, "Bring up two or three jars."

"He drank four yesterday, Mrs. Bean."

"Yes, but he won't want that many today because he's not going to be up there more than a few hours longer. He says the fox is bound to make a run for it this morning. It can't possibly stay down that hole another day without food."

The woman in the cellar reached out and lifted a jar of cider from the shelf. The jar she took was next but one to the jar behind which Mr. Fox was crouching.

"I'll be glad when the rotten brute is killed and strung up on the front porch," she called out. "And by the way, Mrs. Bean, your husband promised I could have the tail as a souvenir."

"The tail's been all shot to pieces," said the voice from upstairs. "Didn't you know that?"

"You mean it's *ruined*?"

"Of course it's ruined. They shot the tail but missed the fox."

"Oh heck!" said the big woman. "I did so want that tail!"

"You can have the head instead, Mabel. You can get it stuffed and hang it on your bedroom wall. Hurry up now with that cider!"

"Yes, Ma'am, I'm coming," said the big woman, and she took a second jar from the shelf.

If she takes one more, she'll see us, thought Mr. Fox. He could feel the Smallest Fox's body pressed tightly against his own, quivering with excitement.

"Will two be enough, Mrs. Bean, or shall I take three?"

"My goodness, Mabel, I don't care so long as you get a move on!"

"Then two it is," said the huge woman, speaking to herself now. "He drinks too much anyway."

Carrying a jar in each hand and with the rolling-pin tucked under one arm, she walked away across the cellar. At the foot of the steps she paused and looked around, sniffing the air. "There's rats down here again, Mrs. Bean. I can smell 'em."

"Then poison them, woman, poison them! You know where the poison's kept."

"Yes, Ma'am," Mabel said. She climbed slowly out of sight up the steps. The door slammed.

"Quick!" said Mr. Fox. "Grab a jar each and run for it!"

Rat stood on his high shelf and shrieked. "What did I tell you! You nearly got nabbed, didn't you? You nearly gave the game away! You keep out of here from now on! I don't want you around! This is my place!"

"*You,*" said Mr. Fox, "are going to be poisoned."

"Poppycock!" said Rat. "I sit up here and watch her putting the stuff down. She'll never get *me.*"

Mr. Fox and Badger and the Smallest Fox ran across the cellar clutching a gallon jar each. "Goodbye, Rat!" they called out as they disappeared through the hole in the wall. "Thanks for the lovely cider!"

"Thieves!" shrieked Rat. "Robbers! Bandits! Burglars!"

17
The Great Feast

BACK IN THE TUNNEL they paused so that Mr. Fox could brick up the hole in the wall. He was humming to himself as he put the bricks back in place. "I can still taste that glorious cider," he said. "What an impudent fellow Rat is."

"He has bad manners," Badger said. "All rats have bad manners. I've never met a polite rat yet."

"And he drinks too much," said Mr. Fox, putting the last brick in place. "There we are. Now, home to the feast!"

They grabbed their jars of cider and off they went. Mr. Fox was in front, the Smallest Fox came next and Badger last. Along the tunnel they flew . . . past the turning that led to Bunce's Mighty Storehouse . . . past Boggis's Chicken House Number One and then up the long home stretch towards the place where they knew Mrs. Fox would be waiting.

"Keep it up, my darlings!" shouted Mr. Fox. "We'll soon be there! Think what's waiting for us at the other end! And just think what we're bringing home with us in these jars! That ought to cheer up poor Mrs. Fox." Mr. Fox sang a little song as he ran:

> *"Home again swiftly I glide,*
> *Back to my beautiful bride.*
> *She'll not feel so rotten*
> *As soon as she's gotten*
> *Some cider inside her inside."*

Then Badger joined in:

> *"Oh poor Mrs. Badger, he cried,*
> *So hungry she very near died.*
> *But she'll not feel so hollow*
> *If only she'll swallow*
> *Some cider inside her inside."*

They were still singing as they rounded the final corner and burst in upon the most wonderful and amazing sight any of them had ever seen. The feast was just beginning. A large dining-room had been hollowed out of the earth, and in the middle of it, seated around a huge table, were no less than twenty-nine animals. They were:

Mrs. Fox and three Small Foxes.

Mrs. Badger and three Small Badgers.

Mole and Mrs. Mole and four Small Moles.

Rabbit and Mrs. Rabbit and five Small Rabbits.

Weasel and Mrs. Weasel and six Small Weasels.

The table was covered with chickens and ducks and geese and hams and bacon, and everyone was tucking into the lovely food.

"My darling!" cried Mrs. Fox, jumping up and hugging Mr. Fox. "We couldn't wait! Please forgive us!" Then she hugged the Smallest Fox of all, and Mrs. Badger hugged Badger, and everyone hugged everyone else. Amid shouts of joy, the great jars of cider were placed upon the table, and Mr. Fox and Badger and the Smallest Fox sat down with the others.

You must remember no one had eaten a thing for several days. They were ravenous. So for a while there was no conversation at all. There was only the sound of crunching and chewing as the animals attacked the succulent food.

At last, Badger stood up. He raised his glass of cider and called out, "A toast! I want you all to stand and drink a toast to our dear friend who has saved our lives this day—Mr. Fox!"

"To Mr. Fox!" they all shouted, standing up and raising their glasses. "To Mr. Fox! Long may he live!"

Then Mrs. Fox got shyly to her feet and said, "I don't want to make a speech. I just want to say one thing, and it is this: MY HUSBAND IS A FANTASTIC FOX." Everyone clapped and cheered. Then Mr. Fox himself stood up.

"This delicious meal . . ." he began, then he stopped. In the silence that followed, he let fly a tremendous belch. There was laughter and more clapping. "This delicious meal, my friends," he went on, "is by courtesy of Messrs Boggis, Bunce and Bean." (More cheering and laughter.) "And I hope you have enjoyed it as much as I have." He let fly another colossal belch.

"Better out than in," said Badger.

"Thank you," said Mr. Fox, grinning hugely. "But now, my friends, let us be serious. Let us think of tomorrow and the next day and the days after that. If we go out, we will be killed. Right?"

"Right!" they shouted.

"We'll be shot before we've gone a yard," said Badger.

"Ex-*actly*," said Mr. Fox. "But who *wants* to go out, anyway; let me ask you that? We are all diggers, every one of us. We hate the outside. The outside is full of enemies. We only go out because we have to, to get food for our families. But now, my friends, we have an entirely new set-up. We have a safe tunnel leading to three of the finest stores in the world!"

"We do indeed!" said Badger. "I've seen 'em!"

"And you know what this means?" said Mr. Fox. *"It means that none of us need ever go out into the open again!"*

There was a buzz of excitement around the table.

"I therefore invite you all," Mr. Fox went on, "to stay here with me for ever."

"For ever!" they cried. "My goodness! How marvellous!" And Rabbit said to Mrs. Rabbit, "My dear, just think! We're never going to be shot at again in our lives!"

"We will make," said Mr. Fox, "a little underground village, with streets and houses on each side—separate houses for Badgers and Moles and Rabbits and Weasels and Foxes. And every day I will go shopping for you all. And every day we will eat like kings."

The cheering that followed this speech went on for many minutes.

18
Still Waiting

OUTSIDE THE FOX'S HOLE, Boggis and Bunce and Bean
sat beside their tents with their guns on their laps. It
was beginning to rain. Water was trickling down the
necks of the three men and into their shoes.

"He won't stay down there much longer now,"
Boggis said.

"The brute must be famished," Bunce said.

"That's right," Bean said. "He'll be making a dash for it any moment. Keep your guns handy."

They sat there by the hole, waiting for the fox to come out.

And so far as I know, they are still waiting.

TURN THE PAGE FOR A LOOK AT ANOTHER SCRUMDIDDLYUMPTIOUS STORY FROM ROALD DAHL!

Noт far from where I live there is a queer old empty wooden house standing all by itself on the side of the road. I long to explore inside it but the door is always locked, and when I peer through a window all I can see is darkness and dust. I know the ground floor used once to be a shop because I can still read the faded lettering across the front which says THE GRUBBER. My mother has told me that in our part of the country in the olden days a grubber was another name for a sweet-shop, and now every time I look at it I think to myself what a lovely old sweet-shop it must have been.

On the shop-window itself somebody has painted in white the words FOR SAIL.

One morning, I noticed that FOR SAIL had been scraped off the shop-window and in its place somebody had painted SOLED. I stood there staring at the new writing and wishing like mad that it had been me who had bought it because then I would have been able to make it into a grubber all over again. I have always longed and longed to own a sweet-shop. The sweet-shop of my dreams would be loaded from top to bottom with Sherbet Suckers and Caramel Fudge and

Russian Toffee and Sugar Snorters and Butter Gum-balls and thousands and thousands of other glorious things like that. Oh boy, what I couldn't have done with that old Grubber shop if it had been mine!

On my next visit to The Grubber, I was standing across the road gazing at the wonderful old building when suddenly an enormous bathtub came sailing out through one of the second-floor windows and crashed right on to the middle of the road!

A few moments later, a white porcelain lavatory pan with the wooden seat still on it came flying out of the same window and landed with a wonderful splintering crash just beside the bathtub. This was followed by a kitchen sink and an empty canary-cage and a four-poster bed and two hot-water bottles and a rocking horse and a sewing-machine and goodness knows what else besides.

It looked as though some madman was ripping out the whole of the inside of the house, because now pieces of staircase and bits of the banisters and a whole lot of old floorboards came whistling through the windows.

Then there was silence. I waited and waited but not another sound came from within the building. I crossed the road and stood right under the windows and called out, "Is anybody at home?"

There was no answer.

In the end it began to get dark so I had to turn away and start walking home. But you can bet your life nothing was going to stop me from hurrying back there again tomorrow morning to see what the next surprise was going to be.

When I got back to the Grubber house the next morning, the first thing I noticed was the new door. The dirty old brown door had been taken out and in its place someone had fitted a brand-new red one. The new door was fantastic. It was twice as high as the other one had been and it looked ridiculous. I couldn't begin to imagine who would want a tremendous tall door like that in his house unless it was a giant.

As well as this, somebody had scraped away the SOLED notice on the shop-window and now there was a whole lot of different writing all over the glass. I stood there reading it and reading it and trying to figure out what on earth it all meant.

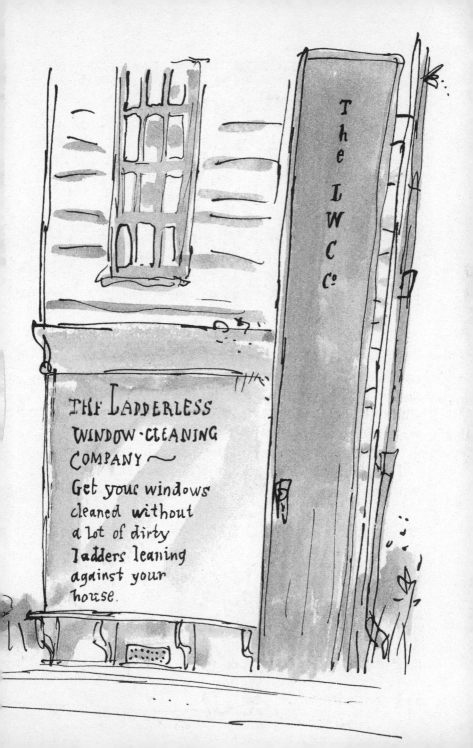

THE LADDERLESS
WINDOW·CLEANING
COMPANY ~
Get your windows
cleaned without
a lot of dirty
ladders leaning
against your
house.

The LWC Co

I tried to catch some sign or sound of movement inside the house but there was none . . . until all of a sudden . . . out of the corner of my eye . . . I noticed that one of the windows on the top floor was slowly beginning to open outwards . . .

Then a HEAD appeared at the open window.

I stared at the head. The head stared back at me with big round dark eyes.

Suddenly, a second window was flung wide open and of all the crazy things a gigantic white bird hopped out and perched on the window-sill. I knew what this

one was because of its amazing beak which was shaped like a huge orange-coloured basin. The Pelican looked down at me and sang out:

> *"Oh, how I wish*
> *For a big fat fish!*
> *I'm as hungry as ever could be!*
> *A dish of fish is my only wish!*
> *How far are we from the sea?"*

"We are a long way from the sea," I called back to him, "but there is a fishmonger in the village not far away."

"A fish *what*?"

"A fish*monger*."

"Now what on earth would that be?" asked the Pelican. "I have heard of a fish-*pie* and a fish-*cake* and a fish-*finger*, but I have never heard of a fish-*monger*. Are these mongers good to eat?"

This question baffled me a bit, so I said, "Who is your friend in the next window?"

"She is the Giraffe!" the Pelican answered. "Is she not wonderful? Her legs are on the ground floor and her head is looking out of the top window!"

As if all this wasn't enough, the window on the *first floor* was now flung wide open and out popped a Monkey!

The Monkey stood on the window-sill and did a jiggly little dance. He was so skinny he seemed to be made only out of furry bits of wire, but he danced wonderfully well, and I clapped and cheered and did a little dance myself in return.

"We are the Window-Cleaners!" sang out the
Monkey.

> "We will polish your glass
> Till it's shining like brass
> And it sparkles like sun on the sea!
> We are quick and polite,
> We will come day or night,
> The Giraffe and the Pelly and me!
>
> We're a fabulous crew,
> We know just what to do,
> And we never stop work to drink tea.
> All your windows will glow
> When we give them a go,
> The Giraffe and the Pelly and me!
>
> We use water and soap
> Plus some kindness and hope,
> But we never use ladders, not we.
> Who needs ladders at all
> When you're thirty feet tall?
> Not Giraffe, and not Pelly! Not me!"

I stood there enthralled. Then I heard the Giraffe saying to the Pelican in the next window, "Pelly, my dear, be so good as to fly down and bring that small person up here to talk to us."

At once the Pelican spread his huge white wings and flew down on to the road beside me. "Hop in," he said, opening his enormous beak.

I stared at the great orange beak and backed away.

"Go ON!" the Monkey shouted from up in his window. "The Pelly isn't going to *swallow* you! Climb IN!"

I said to the Pelican, "I'll only get in if you promise not to shut your beak once I'm inside."

"You have nothing to fear!" cried the Pelican,

"And let me tell you why.
I have a very special beak!
A special beak have I!
You'll never see a beak so fine,
I don't care where you go.
There's magic in this beak of mine!
Hop in and don't say NO!"

"I will *not* hop in," I said, "unless you swear on your honour you won't shut it once I'm inside. I don't like small dark places."

"When I have done what I am just about to do," said the Pelican, "I won't be *able* to shut it. You don't seem to understand how my beak works."

"Show me," I said.

"Watch this!" cried the Pelican.

I watched in amazement as the top half of the Pelican's beak began to slide smoothly backwards into his head until the whole thing was almost out of sight.

"It bends and goes down inside the back of my neck!" cried the Pelican. "Is that not sensible? Is it not magical?"

"It's unbelievable," I said. "It's exactly like one of those metal tape-measures my father's got at home. When it's out, it's straight. When you slide it back in, it bends and disappears."

"Precisely," said the Pelican. "You see, the top half is of no use to me unless I am chewing fish. The bottom half is what counts, my lad! The bottom half of this glorious beak of mine is the bucket in which we carry our window-cleaning water! So if I didn't slide the top half away I'd be standing around all day long holding it open!

"So I slide it away
For the rest of the day!
Even so, I'm still able to speak!
And wherever I've flown
It has always been known
As the Pelican's Patented Beak!

If I want to eat fish
(That's my favourite dish)
All I do is I give it a tweak!
In the blink of an eye
Out it pops! And they cry,
'It's the Pelican's Patented Beak!'"

STORIES ARE GOOD FOR YOU.

Roald Dahl said,
*"If you have good thoughts, they will shine
out of your face like sunbeams and you
will always look lovely."*

We believe in doing good things.
That's why 10 percent of all Roald Dahl income*
goes to our charity partners. We have supported
causes including: specialist children's nurses, grants for
families in need, and educational outreach programs.
Thank you for helping us to sustain this vital work.

Find out more at roalddahl.com